Ladybird I'm **Ready...** for Phonics!

Note to parents, carers and teachers

Ladybird I'm Ready for Phonics is a series of phonic reading books that have been carefully written to give gradual, structured practice of the synthetic phonics programme your child is learning at school.

Each book focuses on a set of phonemes (sounds) together with their graphemes (letters). The books also provide practice of common tricky words, such as **the** and **said**, that cannot be sounded out.

The series closely follows the order that your child is taught phonics in school, from initial letter sounds to key phonemes and beyond. It helps to build reading confidence through practice of these phonics building blocks, and reinforces school learning in a fun way.

Ideas for use

- Children learn best when reading is a fun experience. Read the book together and give your child plenty of praise and encouragement.

- Help your child identify and sound out the phonemes (sounds) in any words she is having difficulty reading. Then, blend these sounds together to read the word.

- Talk about the story words, high-frequency words and tricky words at the end of the stories to reinforce learning.

For more information and advice on synthetic phonics and school book banding, visit **www.ladybird.com/phonics**

Book
Band
4

Level 11 builds on the phonics learning covered in levels 1 to 10 and focuses on alternative spellings for the sounds learnt in previous levels.

Special features:

repetition of sounds with alternative spellings

short sentences with simple language

Come to Wizard Woody's cave,
if you need a super spell.
Wizard Woody's wise and brave,
but he can not hear too well...

6

7

Story Words

Can you match up these rhyming words with their pairs?

snakes   baboon   fly

cakes   tune

cry   bee   tea

16

Tricky Words

These tricky words are in the story you have just read. They cannot be phonetically sounded out. Can you memorize them and read them super fast?

come

one

out

17

summary page to reinforce learning

Written by Catherine Baker
Illustrated by Ian Cunliffe

Phonics and Book Banding Consultant: Kate Ruttle

A catalogue record for this book is available from the British Library

Published by Ladybird Books Ltd
80 Strand, London, WC2R 0RL
A Penguin Company

001

ISBN: 978-0-72327-547-3
Printed in China

Ladybird I'm Ready... for Phonics!

Wizard Woody's Cave

Come to Wizard Woody's cave,
if you need a super spell.
Wizard Woody's wise and brave,
but he can not hear too well...

If you wish for cakes to eat,
you may end up with snakes for feet.

If you wish for a pet baboon,
you might end up with a silly tune.

If you need a spell to make you fly,
you might get one to make you cry.

If you just need a cup of tea,
you may get stung by a bumblebee.

If you go to Wizard Woody's cave,
you must be wise, as well as brave.
Spell out the thing you really need,
and note it down for him to read!

Story Words

Can you match up these rhyming words with their pair?

snakes

baboon

fly

cakes

tune

cry

bee

tea

Tricky Words

These tricky words are in the story you have just read. They cannot be phonetically sounded out. Can you memorize them and read them super fast?

come

one

out

Ladybird I'm Ready...
for Phonics!

Woody to the Rescue

If you have a big problem,
and you can not sort it out,
you can call on Wizard Woody.
Tell him what it's all about!

21

When he gets a call for help,
he grabs his super cloak.
He shoots up into the air,
in a cloud of super smoke.

If you need a fire put out,
he will quickly do it.
He will squirt it with his blaster pack,
there's really nothing to it.

It's Woody to the rescue,
if a cat's stuck in a tree.
And if the owner's stuck as well,
Woody will set her free!

If you call for Woody's help,
he always tries his best.
But when he gets back to his cave,
he needs a little rest!

cloud

tree

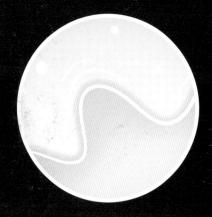

cricket

twirl

Tricky Words

These tricky words are in the story you have just read. They cannot be phonetically sounded out. Can you memorize them and read them super fast?

when

do

out

what

have

there

Collect all
Ladybird I'm Ready...
for Phonics!

Captain Comet's Space Party

9780723275374

Nat Naps!

9780723275381

Top Dog

9780723275398

Huff! Puff! Run!

9780723275404

Fix It Vets

9780723275411

Dash is Fab!

9780723275428

Big, Big Fish

9780723275435

Dig, Farmer, Dig!

9780723275442

Fun Fair Fun

9780723275459

Wow, Wowzer!

9780723275466

Wizard Woody

9780723275473

Monster Stars

9780723275480

Say the Sounds

9780723271598

Flashcards

9780723272069